Paddington's Disappearing Trick

written by Michael Bond
illustrated by Nick Ward for Ross Design

Young Lions
An Imprint of HarperCollinsPublishers

First published in Great Britain 1992 in Young Lions
3 5 7 9 8 6 4 2

Young Lions is an imprint of the Children's Division,
part of HarperCollins Publishers Ltd,
77–85 Fulham Palace Road, Hammersmith,
London W6 8JB

ISBN 0 00 674416-8

Printed and bound in Great Britain by
HarperCollins Manufacturing, Glasgow

Part One

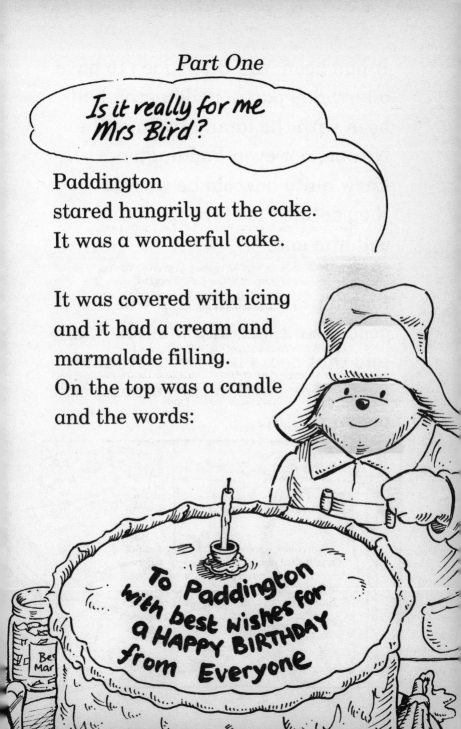

Is it really for me Mrs Bird?

Paddington
stared hungrily at the cake.
It was a wonderful cake.

It was covered with icing
and it had a cream and
marmalade filling.
On the top was a candle
and the words:

To Paddington
with best wishes for
a HAPPY BIRTHDAY
from Everyone

It had been Mrs Bird's idea to have a birthday party. Paddington had been with the family two months. No one, not even Paddington, knew quite how old he was, so they decided to start again and call him one.

Paddington thought this was a good idea, especially when he was told that bears had two birthdays every year - one in the summer and one in winter.

Just like the Queen. So you ought to consider yourself very important.

Paddington did.

In fact he went round to Mr Gruber straight away and told him the good news. Mr Gruber looked most impressed and he was pleased when Paddington invited him to the party.

It's not often anyone invites me out Mr Brown. I don't know when I went out last. I shall look forward to it very much.

PLEASE COME TO MY PARTY

He didn't say any more at the time, but the next morning a van drew up outside the Browns' house and delivered a mysterious-looking parcel from all the shopkeepers in the Portobello Market.

They opened the parcel and looked inside.

Aren't you a lucky bear

It was a nice new shopping basket on wheels, with a bell on the side that Paddington could ring to let people know he was coming.

Paddington scratched his head.

"It's a job to know what to do first," he said, as he carefully placed the basket with his other presents. "I shall have a lot of thank you letters to write.'

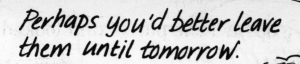

> Perhaps you'd better leave them until tomorrow.

Paddington looked disappointed. He liked writing letters, but he generally managed to get more ink on himself than on the paper.

Today he was looking unusually smart after his bath, so it seemed a pity to spoil it.

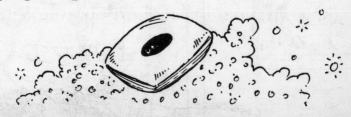

Perhaps I can help, Mrs Bird?

At that moment, Mrs Bird came out of the kitchen.

She had bitter memories of other occasions when Paddington had 'helped' in the kitchen.

I'm glad to say that I've just finished. You can lick the spoons if you like, but not too much...

Or you won't have room for this!

Then Paddington saw his cake for the first time. His eyes, usually large and round, became so much larger and rounder, that even Mrs Bird blushed with pride.

"Special occasions demand special things," she said, and hurried off to the dining room.

Part Two

Paddington spent the rest of the day being hurried from one part of the house to another as preparations were made for his party.

Mrs Brown was busy tidying up. Mrs Bird was busy in the kitchen. Jonathan and Judy were busy with the decorations. Everyone had a job except Paddington.

"I thought it was supposed to be *my* birthday," he grumbled, as he was sent packing into the drawing-room for the fifth time after upsetting a box of marbles over the kitchen floor.

So it is, dear, but your time comes later.

Mrs Brown was beginning to regret telling him that bears had two birthdays every year. Paddington was already worrying about when the next one was due.

But Paddington didn't seem very keen on this.

"You could practise your conjuring tricks for this evening,' she said.

Among Paddington's many presents was a conjuring set from Mr and Mrs Brown. It was a very expensive one from Barkridges. It had a special magic table,

a large mystery box which made things disappear if you followed the instructions properly,

a magic wand

and several packs of cards.

Paddington emptied them all over the floor and settled down in the middle to read the book of instructions.

He sat there for a long time,
studying the pictures and
diagrams, and reading everything
twice to make sure.

Every now and then, he
absent-mindedly dipped a paw
into his marmalade pot, and
then remembering that there was
a big birthday tea to come, he
reached up and stood
the jar on the magic
table before returning
to his studies.

Best
Marmal

chapter I.

⭐ SPELLS ⭐

How to wave your
magic wand:

1) Swing your
wand forward
2) Turn in a
tight circle

The correct
way to say:

ABRACADABRA!

Paddington stood up clutching the book in one paw, and waved the wand several times through the air.

He also tried saying

ABCA—ABDAB...
ABRACHDABRA!

He looked round. Nothing seemed to have changed, and he was just about to try again, when his eyes nearly popped out of his head.

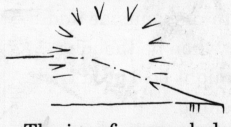

The jar of marmalade, which he'd put on the magic table only a few minutes before - had disappeared!

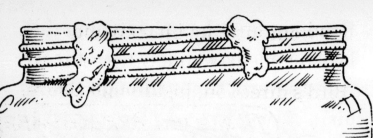

He searched through the book.
There was nothing about making
marmalade disappear.

Worse still, there was nothing
about making it come back again,
either. Paddington decided it must
be a very powerful spell to make
the whole pot vanish into thin air.

He was about to rush outside and
tell the others, when he thought
better of it. It might be a good trick
to do in the evening.

He went into the kitchen and
waved his wand a few times in Mrs
Bird's direction, just to make sure.

*I'll give you ABRACADABRA.
And be careful with that
stick or you'll have
someone's eye
out.*

Paddington went back to the
drawing-room and tried saying his
spell backwards.

ARBADACARBA?

Nothing happened,
so he started reading
the next chapter of
the instruction book,
which was called
*The Mystery of the
Disappearing Egg.*

Part Three

At lunchtime, Paddington told everyone all about it.

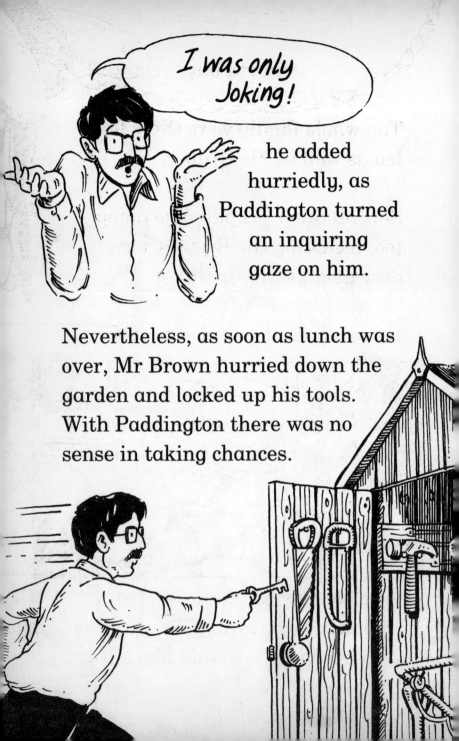

I was only Joking!

he added hurriedly, as Paddington turned an inquiring gaze on him.

Nevertheless, as soon as lunch was over, Mr Brown hurried down the garden and locked up his tools. With Paddington there was no sense in taking chances.

Part Four

The whole family were there for tea as well as Mr Gruber.

Several other people came along too, including the Browns' next door neighbour, Mr Curry.

He was a most unwelcome visitor.

"Just because there's a free tea. I think it's disgusting. He's not even been invited," said Mrs Bird.

"After all the things he's said in the past! And he hasn't even bothered to wish Paddington a happy birthday," said Mr Brown.

Mr Curry had a reputation for meanness and for poking his nose into other people's business. He was also very bad-tempered, and was always complaining, especially about Paddington, which was why the Browns had not invited him to the party.

But even Mr Curry couldn't complain about the tea. From the huge birthday cake down to the last marmalade sandwich, everyone voted it the best tea they had ever had.

Paddington was so full, he had great difficulty in taking a deep enough breath to blow out the candle.

But at last he managed it ,without burning his whiskers. And everyone, including Mr Curry, applauded and wished him a happy birthday.

Part Five

While everyone was busy moving
their seats to one side of the room,
Paddington disappeared into the
drawing-room and returned
carrying his conjuring outfit.

There was a short delay while he
put up his mystery table,

and adjusted
the mystery box,

but soon all was ready.

The lights were turned off except
for one. Paddington waved his
wand for quiet.

Paddington ignored the remark
and turned over the page.

"For this trick," he said," I shall
require an egg."

" Oh dear," said Mrs Bird, as she hurried out to the kitchen,

I know something dreadful is going to happen.

Paddington placed the egg in the centre of his magic table and covered it with a handkerchief.

He muttered ABRACADABRA several times, then hit the handkerchief with his wand.

Mr and Mrs Brown looked at each other. They were both thinking of their carpet.

"Hey presto!" said Paddington, and pulled the handkerchief away.

To everyone's surprise, the egg had completely disappeared.

Everyone clapped loudly.

Of course, it's all done by sleight of paw. But very good though – for a bear. Very good indeed! Now make it come back again!

Paddington was feeling very pleased with himself. He took his bow and then felt in the secret compartment behind the table.

To his surprise, he found something much larger than an egg

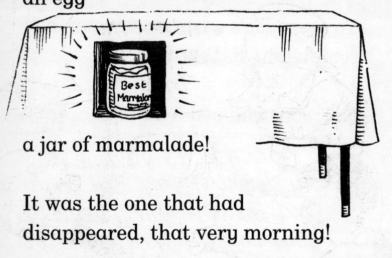

a jar of marmalade!

It was the one that had disappeared, that very morning!

He displayed it in his paw.

The applause for this trick was even louder.

"Excellent," said Mr Curry, slapping his knee. "Making people think he was going to find an egg, and it was a jar of marmalade all the time. Very good indeed!"

Paddington turned over a page.

He took a bowl of Mrs Brown's best flowers and placed them on the dining-table next to his mystery box.

He wasn't very happy about this trick, as he hadn't time to practise it. He wasn't at all sure how the mystery box worked or even where you put the flowers to make them disappear.

He opened the door in the back of the box and poked his head round the side.

he said, then disappeared from view again.

The audience sat in silence. After a while Mr Curry muttered:

He got up, knocked loudly on the box, and then put his ear to it.

"I can hear someone calling," he said. "It sounds like Paddington. I'll try again."

He shook the box. There was an answering thump from inside.

THUMP

"I think he's shut himself in," said
Mr Gruber. He too knocked on the
box.

said a small and muffled voice.
"It's dark and I can't read my
instruction book."

Part Six

Later, after they had prised open Paddington's mystery box with a pen-knife, Mr Curry helped himself to some biscuits.

Paddington looked at him
suspiciously. But Mr Curry was
busy with the biscuits.

"Are you sure?" asked Mrs Brown anxiously. "Wouldn't anything else do?"

Paddington consulted his instruction book.

It says a watch.

he said firmly.

Mr Brown hurriedly pulled his sleeve down over his left wrist.

Unfortunately, Mr Curry, who was in an unusually good mood after his free tea, stood up and offered his watch.

Paddington took it gratefully and placed it on the table.

"This is a jolly good trick," he said, reaching down into his box and pulling out a small hammer.

He covered the watch with a handkerchief and...

hit it several times!

THWACK

Paddington looked rather worried.
He'd just turned over the page and
read the ominous words:

It is necessary to have a
second watch for this trick.

Gingerly, he lifted up the corner of
the handkerchief.

Several cogs and some pieces of
glass rolled across the table.

Mr Curry let out a roar of wrath.

"I think I forgot to say ABRACADABRA," faltered Paddington.

"ABRACADABRA!" shouted Mr Curry, beside himself with rage. *"ABRACADABRA!"*

He held up the remains of his watch.

Twenty years I've had this watch and now _look_ at it! This will cost someone a pretty penny.

Mr Gruber took out an eyeglass and examined the watch carefully.

"Nonsense," he said, coming to Paddington's rescue. "It's one you bought from me for fifty pence six months ago! You ought to be ashamed of yourself, telling lies in front of a young bear!"

"Rubbish!" spluttered Mr Curry. He sat down heavily on Paddington's chair. "Rubbish! I'll give you..." His voice trailed away and a peculiar expression came over his face.

Mr Curry grew purple in the face.

He turned at the door and waved an accusing finger. "It's the last time I shall ever come to one of *your* birthday parties."

The door closed behind him.

Part Seven

"Henry," said Mrs Brown, "you really shouldn't laugh."

Mr Brown tried hard to keep a straight face. "It's no good, "he said, bursting out. "I can't help it."

"Did you see his face when all the cogs rolled out?" said Mr Gruber, his face wet with tears.

"Yes, that sounds like a nice quiet one," said Mrs Brown. "Let's see that."

You wouldn't like another disappearing trick?

"Quite sure, dear," said Mrs Brown.

"Well," said Paddington, rummaging in his box, "it's not very easy doing card tricks when you've only got paws, but I don't mind trying."

He offered a pack of cards to Mr Gruber, who solemnly took one from the middle, looked at it and gave it back.

Paddington waved his wand over the pack

ABRACADABRA

then picked a card.

He held up the seven of spades.

Was this it?

"This is the difficult bit," said Paddington, tearing it up. "I'm not very sure about this part.

He put the pieces under his handkerchief and tapped them several times with the wand.

"Oh!" said Mr Gruber, rubbing the side of his head. "I felt something go pop in my ear just then. Something cold and hard."

He felt in his ear.

He held up a shining round object

"It's a pound coin! My birthday
present for Paddington! Now I
wonder how it got there?"

Oooh. I didn't
expect that. Thank
you very much.
Mr Gruber.

"Well," said Mr Gruber. "It's only a
small present I'm afraid, Mr
Brown. But I've enjoyed the little
chats we've had in the mornings
and.. er.."

He cleared his throat and looked around,

When the chorus of agreement had
died down, Mr Brown rose and
looked at his watch.

And now it's long past our
bedtimes - most of all yours
Paddington, so I suggest
we all do a
disappearing trick
now!

Paddington, stood at the door
waving everyone goodbye,
" I should like to write thank
you letters to every one." he said.

Mrs Brown took his paw.
" In the morning, " she said,
hastily. "You've got clean sheets,
remember."

Yes, in the morning
I expect if I did it now
I'd get ink on the sheets
or something. Things are
always happening to me.

Paddington
went up the stairs to
bed, looking rather
sticky and more than a little
sleepy.

You know, Henry,
it's nice having a
bear about the house.